A CHRISTMAS STORY

BRIAN WILDSMITH

Oxford University Press
Oxford Toronto Melbourne

Once, a long time ago, in a town called Nazareth, a little donkey was born.

When the little donkey was almost nine months old, his mother set out on a long journey with her mistress and master, whose names were Mary and Joseph.

They asked Rebecca, who lived next door to them, to look after the little donkey while they were gone.

But the little donkey was very sad without his mother and refused to eat.
So Rebecca packed food and water and promised the little donkey that they

would find his mother. And they set out to follow Mary and Joseph.

The roads were full of people travelling to various towns and cities.
'Have you seen a donkey with a man and a woman?' Rebecca asked a traveller.
'Yes, they passed me on the road to Jerusalem,' the traveller replied.

Rebecca and the little donkey took the road to Jerusalem. Soon they came to a soldier standing guard at a splendid palace.

'Have you seen a donkey with a man and a woman?' Rebecca asked the soldier.

'Yes, they passed this way,' the soldier answered. 'Now hurry along. There are important visitors here to see King Herod.'

Rebecca and the little donkey continued on their way. In time, they met some shepherds keeping watch over their flocks.
'Have you seen a donkey with a man and a woman?' Rebecca asked them.

'Yes, they were going towards Bethlehem,' the shepherds replied.

So the little donkey and Rebecca went on. Suddenly glorious
music filled the sky. And then they saw a great star shining
down on the little town of Bethlehem.

When they reached Bethlehem, they met a man standing in the
doorway of an inn. Rebecca asked if he had seen Mary and
Joseph and the donkey.
'Yes,' he replied. 'They wanted to stay here, but there was no
room at the inn. They went to the stable.' And the innkeeper
showed Rebecca the way.

The stable was bathed in a wonderful light that shone from the bright star above.
As Rebecca and the little donkey came near, they heard the sounds of a mother donkey braying and a little baby crying.

Rebecca and the little donkey entered the stable and saw Mary
and Joseph and the mother donkey. And there, lying in a
manger, was a new-born baby.

'What are you going to call him?' asked Rebecca.
'His name is Jesus,' Mary replied.

In the days that followed, the little donkey and his mother went with Mary and Joseph and the baby Jesus into Egypt. And Rebecca rode home on a king's camel.

And it came to pass that Mary and Joseph returned to Nazareth, and there
Jesus grew up, with Rebecca as his friend.

FOR LITTLE ORNELLA

Oxford University Press, Walton Street, Oxford OX2 6DP
Oxford is a trade mark of Oxford University Press
© Brian Wildsmith 1989
First published 1989   Reprinted 1989, 1990
First published as paperback 1991
Printed in Hong Kong

Hardback ISBN 0 19 279872 3   Paperback ISBN 0 19 272244 1
British Library Cataloguing in Publication Data
Wildsmith, Brian
A Christmas Story
I. Title
823'.914[J]